Yosef's Dream

Written by Sylvia Rouss

with Ambassador Asher Naim

Illustrated by Tamar Blumenfeld

This **PJ BOOK** belongs to

_____

_____

PJ Library®

JEWISH BEDTIME STORIES and SONGS

APPLES & HONEY PRESS

Springfield, NJ · Jerusalem

Dedicated to all those who made
the courageous journey

Text copyright © 2016 by Sylvia Rouss and Asher Naim
Illustrations copyright © 2016 by Tamar Blumenfeld

The sign outside the school on page 24 means "May God bless you with health" and is commonly used as "Hello" or "Nice to meet you."

Published by Apples & Honey Press
An imprint of Behrman House and Gefen Publishing House
Behrman House, 11 Edison Place, Springfield, New Jersey 07081
Gefen Publishing House Ltd., 6 Hatzvi Street, Jerusalem 94386, Israel
www.applesandhoneypress.com

ISBN 978- 1-68115-506-7

Names: Rouss, Sylvia A., author. | Naim, Asher, author.
Title: Yosef's dream / by Sylvia Rouss and Asher Naim.
Description: Springfield, New Jersey : Apples & Honey Press, an imprint of Behrman House and Gefen Publishing House, [2016] |
Summary: "Now a young man in Israel, watching his brother become a Bar Mitzvah, Yosef remembers back to his own childhood
in Ethiopia, and the dream he had, foreseeing the miraculous air rescue of Operation Solomon in 1991, which led to the fulfillment
of his own family's dream to live in Israel, land of their forefathers"-- Provided by publisher.
Identifiers: LCCN 2014048815 | ISBN 9781681155067
Subjects: LCSH: Operation Solomon, 1991--Juvenile fiction. | Jews--Ethiopia--Juvenile fiction. | CYAC: Operation Solomon,
1991--Fiction. | Jews--Ethiopia--Fiction. | Blacks--Ethiopia--Fiction. | Ethiopia--History--20th century--Fiction.
Classification: LCC PZ7.R7622 Yo 2016 | DDC [E]--dc23 LC record available at http://lccn.loc.gov/2014048815

Printed in China
2 4 6 8 10 9 7 5 3 1
041715.7K1/B0822/A8

"Those with hope in God will renew their strength;

they will soar aloft as with eagles' wings."

(From Isaiah 40:31)

The Western Wall glints in the early morning Jerusalem sunlight. We watch proudly as my younger brother, Jacob, chants the Hebrew prayers. Today is his bar mitzvah—and he is becoming a man.

It is a long time since we left our small African village.

I was just a boy....

I still remember the tall mountains, flowing rivers, and wide plains that were also home to baboons, hippos, and herds of zebra. My people had lived in Ethiopia for thousands of years, but we were still seen as strangers, for we were Jewish...and different.

For a long time, we thought we were the only Jews left in the world! It was only when my great-grandfather was a boy that we learned that others like us lived in faraway places—like Israel. Every Shabbat and holy day, when we gathered in our synagogue to listen to our rabbi, we prayed to return to the land of our ancestors.

In the evenings, my family would gather outside our small hut and eat together—my father and mother, my sister and brother, and me.

We loved Friday nights best. My mother would make the spicy meat stew that my father loved most, and we'd laugh and joke while sitting around the fire. Later, as we lay on our mats, we listened to stories our parents told us of long ago as the stars shone their light through the open doorway.

Suddenly, I am a young boy again....

It is morning, and my mother is saying, "Yosef, wake up!" I squirm as she tickles my bare feet. "An important visitor is coming to school today. You must not be late!"

A visitor?

Yawning, I get up and dress quickly.

I can smell the injera bread my sister, Minya, is baking outside. Minya is a big help to my mother. Besides cooking, she also weaves the baskets and makes the pottery that my family sells in the market. As I look at my mother's rounded belly, I know that she will soon rely on my sister even more.

Outside, I reach for a piece of the warm spongy bread. Minya
snatches it away. "You haven't brushed your teeth!" she scolds. I grab
a twig and scrape it across my teeth. Satisfied, Minya gives me the bread.

I can't wait for the baby to come. Then I will no longer be the youngest! I quickly swallow the last bite of bread and pick up the basket of food to take to my father and brother working in the fields.

I race to where Ezra is herding our sheep, when suddenly

I fall into a deep hole.

I cannot climb out—the sides are too steep! I call for help, but no one answers! What can I do? I gaze up at the clouds overhead....

And then I must have fallen asleep, for Gazelle is peering down into the hole.

"Yosef!" she bleats. "Hold onto my horns, and I will pull you out. If you jump onto my back, I will take you to the tops of tall mountains so you can see far-off places. Each day we will find new mountains to climb."

Her soft voice is interrupted by Hyena's snarl. "No!" he barks. "Grab hold of my tail, Yosef! Together we will hide in the shadows and feed off of the scraps of others. One place is much like another."

All of a sudden, big flapping wings brush Hyena aside.

Eagle, with his great yellow eyes and hooked beak, stares down at me.

"Yosef, pull yourself out!" he cries. "You can do it if you try. Catch hold of my wings, and we will fly to your new home far, far away."

"Hurry! We haven't much time. Wake up, Yosef!"

I open my eyes to find Ezra looking down at me. "Yosef, are you hurt?" he shouts. "I have been calling and calling you. Here, take my hand!"

"I can climb out on my own," I say. I find a small toehold and brace myself, then grab onto clumps of grass and slowly pull myself up.

"Ezra!" I say breathlessly at the top. "I had a dream. Eagle spoke to me!"

But Ezra isn't listening. He takes some food then says, "Hurry and take the rest to Father."

I run to where my father is plowing.

"Father, I'm sorry I am late! I fell into a hole and couldn't get out.
Then I had a strange dream. Would you like to hear it?"

"Later," he smiles. "Run off to school now!"

I hug him and race across the fields! When I arrive at school,
everyone is gathered around a stranger.

My friend, Desta, whispers, "He is Mr. Am-bas-sa-dor. He came all the way from Israel to talk to us!"

Mr. Ambassador tells us something we can't believe!

"Israel is offering all of you a home," he says. "If you want, you can return to the land God gave to the Jews."

If we want?! Of course we do!

An older boy says, "Our legend says that one day we will return to Israel on the wings of eagles."

"Just like my dream!" I exclaim. This time everyone listens. When I finish, Mr. Ambassador asks, "Have you heard of Joseph?"

"Of course!" I nod. "He was a young Hebrew boy who saw the future in his dreams."

"Yes," Mr. Ambassador smiles. "And perhaps, like that Joseph, your dream will come true."

On my way home from school, I search the sky for eagles. I see none.

But I will look again tomorrow. When I reach our hut, men are gathered around my father.

"Soon, we will leave for Jerusalem!" one man says, excitedly.

"I do not believe it will happen," says another.

"Why not?" asks a third man. "You heard the ambassador."

My father frowns. "Our government will never let us go, and anyway," he adds, looking at me, "your mother will soon give birth. How can we go?"

Over the next weeks the villagers prepare for the big trip, hoping it will happen soon. But we do nothing.

One day, Minya shows my father the new basket she has woven.

"If we decide to go to Israel, we can pack our belongings in it," she says, smiling.

"Your mother can't travel now," my father replies. "I'm sorry."

My mother looks up from her weaving then says softly, "Please. Do not deny our children the chance of a better life in our promised land."

"Are you sure you can make this trip?" my father asks. When my mother nods, his face fills with pride.

"Then we shall go!"

One week later, Mr. Ambassador sends us a message that Israel has reached an agreement with the Ethiopian government.

We can leave...but it must be today! TODAY?

My mother quickly packs our belongings, and we put on our fine Shabbat clothes. But before we say good-bye to our home, my father hands each of us a new pair of shoes, saying, "I traded the sheep for these!"

Soon, big long buses come, and we all crowd aboard. We travel nearly all day; finally we stop in a huge open field. The sun is setting when I hear the sky roaring and see an enormous winged bird.

"An eagle!" I shout, as the bird swoops down. "LOOK!"

"No, Yosef. That's an airplane," my father says, smiling.

But I know it is the eagle from my dream. Soon more "eagles" arrive. Hundreds of us line up to climb into the bellies of the giant birds.

High up in the sky, my mother clutches at her stomach. "It is time," she whispers to my father. And there, inside the eagle, my mother gives birth to Jacob, my new baby brother....

Today, thirteen years later, we live in the south of Israel.

My father works on a farm near our home. Ezra, who always had a way with animals, is now a veterinarian. And Minya, with my mother, owns a small shop selling baskets and pottery. As for me—I love this land and its language. I am studying to be a writer.

But today, we are celebrating!

My brother Jacob's bar mitzvah speech is about that dream I had so long ago.

He stands tall as he looks at us and says: "My brother Yosef's dream was about making a choice. If we had gone with Gazelle, my family could have traveled to other countries, never settling anywhere. Had we stayed with Hyena, we would still be living as outcasts in Ethiopia. But we chose to fly with Eagle, and after nearly three thousand years of exile we have returned to Israel, our true home."

AUTHOR'S NOTE

The Jews of Ethiopia lived in isolation for nearly three thousand years. Until quite recently, they believed they were the last remaining Jews in the world. Often oppressed by their Ethiopian hosts, they were outcasts and treated like unwelcome strangers. They were often blamed for droughts, famines, and illnesses. For thousands of years, Ethiopian Jews held onto the hope that one day they would return to Israel. That hope became a reality. Through the efforts of the Israeli government and Asher Naim, the Israeli ambassador to Ethiopia, a stunning rescue mission called Operation Solomon was organized. On May 24, 1991, thirty-four planes, many of them with their seats removed to accommodate as many people as possible, flew more than fourteen thousand Ethiopian Jews to Israel within thirty-six hours. During the flights, seven children were born. I am grateful to Ambassador Naim, with whose help this story was written.

Sylvia Rouss